Try something new.

I know I made a wrong choice.

Next time you'll choose better.

comfort zone.

Surprise someone with kindness.

I'm sorry I hurt your feelings.

I accept your apology.

At first we didn't like each other.

Be a bright light to those around you.

Now we're best friends.

Be open-minded.

I notice you hardly ever complain.

...tions instead.

I lik...

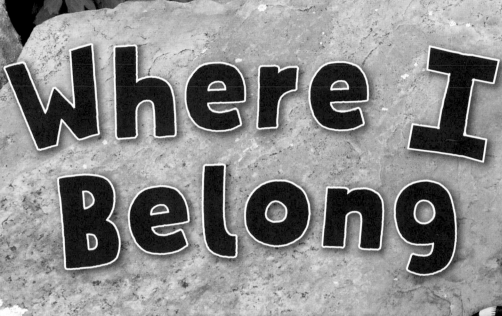

Where I Belong

LINDA KRANZ

Photographs by KLAUS KRANZ

TAYLOR TRADE PUBLISHING
Lanham · Boulder · New York · London

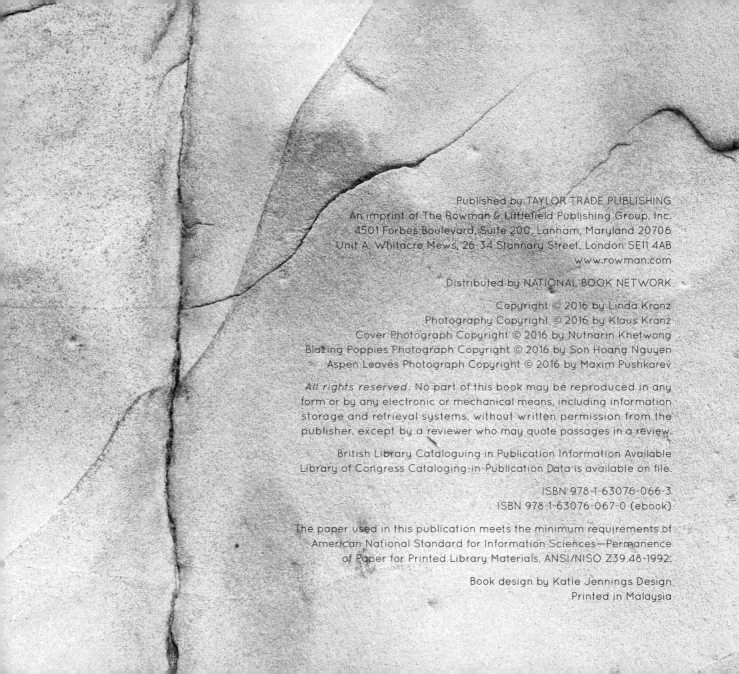

Published by TAYLOR TRADE PUBLISHING
An imprint of The Rowman & Littlefield Publishing Group, Inc.
4501 Forbes Boulevard, Suite 200, Lanham, Maryland 20706
Unit A, Whitacre Mews, 26-34 Stannary Street, London SE11 4AB
www.rowman.com

Distributed by NATIONAL BOOK NETWORK

British Library Cataloguing in Publication Information Available
Library of Congress Cataloging-in-Publication Data is available on file.

ISBN 978-1-63076-066-3
ISBN 978-1-63076-067-0 (ebook)

The paper used in this publication meets the minimum requirements of
American National Standard for Information Sciences—Permanence
of Paper for Printed Library Materials, ANSI/NISO Z39.48-1992.

Book design by Katie Jennings Design
Printed in Malaysia

"Here we are, safe and sound," said Grandfather.
"I can't wait for our next outing."

"Neither can we!" shouted all the snakes together.

Grandfather looked thoughtfully at each snake for a moment and asked, "What did you like best about today?"

"I liked it when we crossed the smooth uneven rocks," said Reed. "They tickled and it made me laugh."

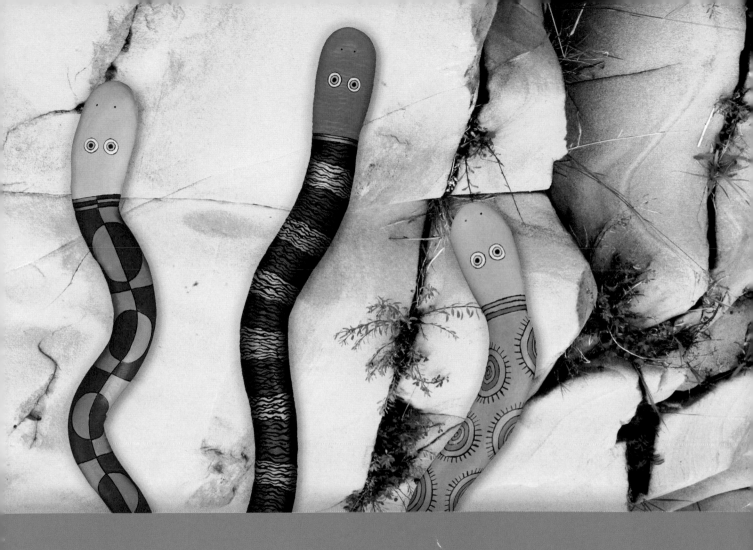

"We all laughed," said Grandfather,
"and laughter is the sound of happiness."

"When we made it across the sand; that's what I liked best," said Holden. "It was hard, but you told us to be patient. You encouraged us the whole way, and we made it through."

"You all persevered.
You never gave up,"
said Grandfather.

"What I liked best," said Charlotte, "was when I got to lead the way. We slid through the cool green meadow during the hottest part of the day. That was soothing."

"I knew you would make a terrific leader," said Marcus, "if you were given the chance."

"The colorful flowers were my favorite part of the day," said Vivian.

"When we stopped and took a break," said Grandfather, "we were able to notice the tiny details in the flowers and enjoy the sweet fragrance in the air."

"I love spending time with all of you and watching you become your own unique selves," said Grandfather.

"How do you know so much?" asked Charlotte.

"Experience, mainly, and by listening and noticing," said Grandfather, as he caught a glimpse of movement out of the corner of his eye.

"So tell us, Maximillian, what was your favorite part of the day?" asked Grandfather.

"Nothing," grumbled Maximillian as he slithered by. "I was following you, but no one paid any attention to me. I need to get away from here and go to a place where I fit in."

"He's on his way to Red Mountain," said Grandfather. "He thinks he'll like it better there, but no one is friendly and no one gets along. I hope he finds what he's looking for, but I think what Maximillian really needs is a friend."

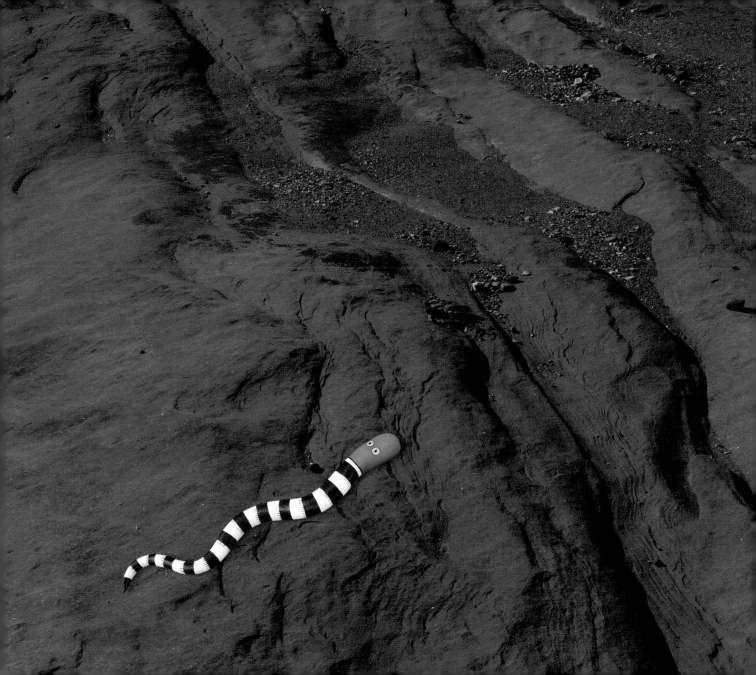

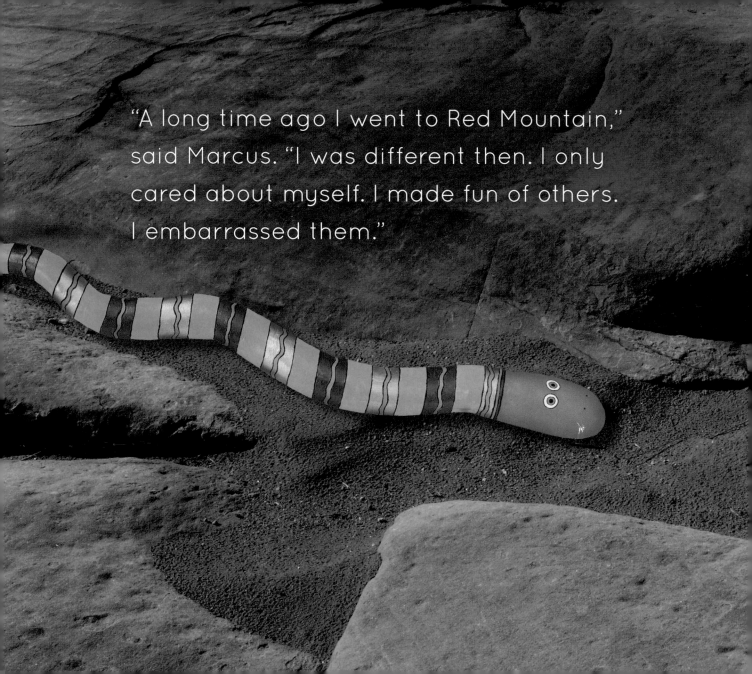

"A long time ago I went to Red Mountain," said Marcus. "I was different then. I only cared about myself. I made fun of others. I embarrassed them."

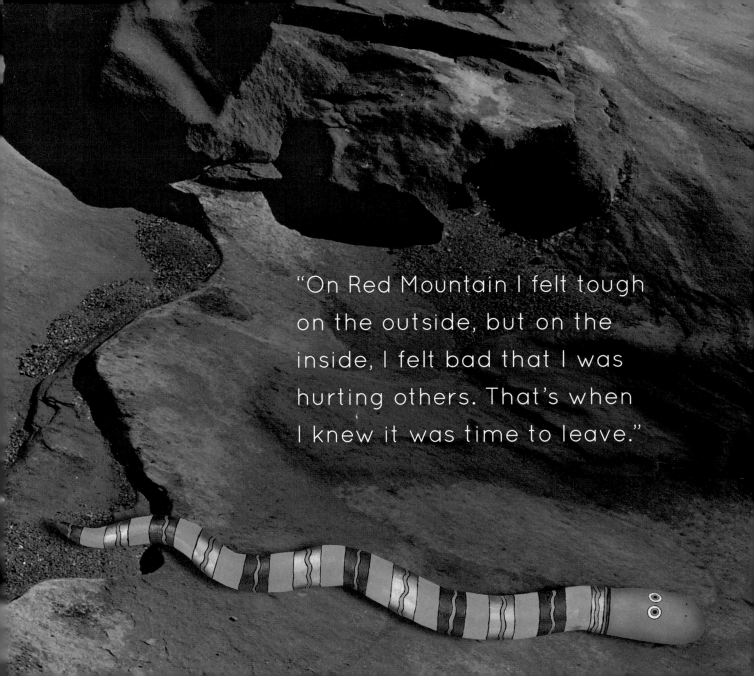

"On Red Mountain I felt tough on the outside, but on the inside, I felt bad that I was hurting others. That's when I knew it was time to leave."

"When I returned, Grandfather noticed I was confused, and we shared many conversations together. He taught me so much.

"Over time, I made new friends. I changed my way of thinking. As for Red Mountain, I never want to see that place again. I hope Maximillian doesn't like it up there."

"Listen," said Marcus. He heard voices off in the distance.

"Hey!" said Vivian. "It's Maximillian."

"Welcome back," said Reed.

"It's good to see you," said Holden and Charlotte together.

"Thanks," said Maximillian. "It's great to be back!"

"What was it like up there?" asked Holden.

"It was awful," said Maximillian with a swoosh of his tail.

"Now I know this is where I belong."

Maximillian introduced the new friends
he met along the way to everyone.

"Why don't all of you join us for a day of
exploring, Maximillian," said Grandfather.

"That sounds like fun," he said. His friends
agreed. "And please, call me Max."

"Yes, come with us," the snakes cheered.

As they gathered together, Grandfather
waited patiently and said,

"If we can all get along and
help each other, the world
will be a place where..."

"we *all* belong."

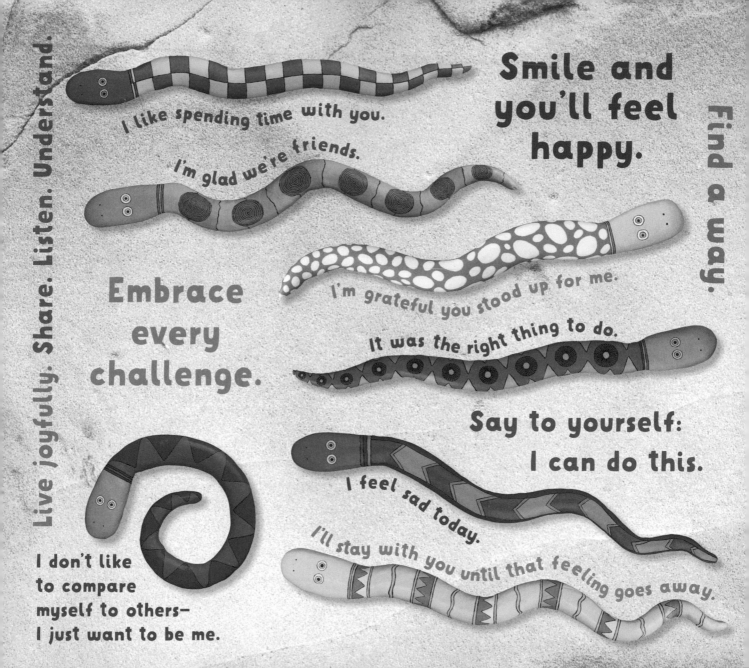